A MAGIC WORD BOOK™

The PEANUT BUTTER and JELLY GAME

by
Adam Eisenson
illustrated by
Joseph Walden

Good Advice Press • Elizaville, New York

In memory of Grandpa Ben, Nanny Bobby, Grandpa Henry,
Rusty, and Christos.
With love to the two best nephews so far, Zack and Josh. – A.E.

To Fiona for her love and great patience, my mother and
father for their endless support and constant prayers.
Thanks to Adam, Marc, and Nancy for their faith and this
great opportunity. – J.W.

Library of Congress Cataloging-in-Publication Data

Eisenson, Adam, 1970-
    The peanut butter and jelly game / written by Adam Eisenson ;
illustrated by Joseph Walden.
        p.   cm.   "A magic word book."
    Summary: Harry the gorilla spends all his grocery money on a new
baseball mitt and then pesters his friends for food.
    ISBN: 0-943973-16-3 (lib. bdg. : alk. paper)
    [1. Gorillas – Fiction. 2. Animals – Fiction. 3. Food habits – Fiction.]
I. Walden, Joseph, 1969- ill. II. Title.
    PZ7.E3467Pe   1996
[E] – dc20   95-41607
                                       CIP
Printed on recycled, acid free paper.   AC

To arrange for author and illustrator appearances or interviews, contact:
Good Advice Press
Box 78
Elizaville, NY 12523
914-758-1400 (phone)   914-758-1475 (fax)

How to Play
The Peanut Butter and Jelly Game

As the reader shares this tale about Harry the Gorilla and his friends, the listeners will wait to hear the magic words, "peanut butter" or "jelly."

Once they're spoken, the children must immediately do something. It can be as simple as clapping their hands 5 times when they hear "jelly," or acting like Harry the Gorilla for a few seconds, in response to "peanut butter."

After the listeners complete the chosen activity, they quickly sit down. When they are quiet, the reader continues the story.

Parents, teachers, and kids can dream up all sorts of responses to the words "peanut butter" and "jelly." For example, the listeners could:

1) Jump up and down 5 times.	6) Write their names.
2) Stand on one foot.	7) Change seats.
3) Raise their right/left hands.	8) Put away one toy.
4) Bring one dish to the table.	9) Say the days of the week.
5) Hold up something that's red.	10) Make an animal noise.

Use *The Peanut Butter and Jelly Game* to:
* Make learning to listen ... fun.
* Exercise the body ... as well as the mind ... away from "the boob tube."
* Invigorate a lethargic child, or help one to work off some excess energy.
* Teach shapes, colors ... anything that would benefit from repetition.
* Encourage family togetherness ... and maybe get help with chores.

Whatever activities you choose or invent, I hope you have a great time playing *The Peanut Butter and Jelly Game.*

– Adam Eisenson

Harry the Gorilla and his best friend, Bradley
the Porcupine, were taking their usual Saturday
drive to the supermarket. On the way, Harry spotted a
sign in the window of Sammy's Sporting Goods Store:
"All Baseball Gloves Half Price."

"Stop the car!" shouted Harry, all excited. "I need a new mitt."

"Harry, you already have one," said Bradley. "What you need is to buy some food ... especially your favorite, peanut butter."

"Yeah, yeah, yeah! But first, I want to check out some baseball gloves. Stop the car!" Harry ordered.

Sammy's had dozens of different mitts, and Harry wanted them all. But he absolutely flipped over the biggest, coolest, and most expensive glove in the store.

"I'm going to get this one," Harry told Bradley. "It's awesome, and what a great deal! It's half off."

"Great deal or not," Bradley warned, "don't blow your grocery money on a mitt you don't need."

"What I don't need is advice from you," Harry sneered. "I can take care of myself."

Having spent every nickel he had on his new glove, Harry sat in the car while Bradley went food shopping. The two best friends were so angry at each other, they didn't talk on the ride home ... or for the next few days.

On Sunday, Monday, and Tuesday, Harry had plenty of peanut butter. Each day he made a thick sandwich of it topped with grape jelly.

Then came Wednesday.

While Harry was watching his favorite TV show, his stomach began to rumble ... and rumble ... and rumble!

Soon, all he could think about was food.

Harry went to the kitchen and opened his refrigerator.
Do you know what he found?

Absolutely nothing!

Bradley had been right. Harry had run out of peanut
butter. The rumbles and growls in the gorilla's stomach
got louder ...

and louder ...

and louder!

Harry had no food, no money ... and no choice. He had to go knock on Bradley's door.

"Who is it?" asked Bradley.

"It's me," answered Harry.

"What do you want?!" Bradley snapped, still mad at Harry. "I'm washing my face and don't want a quill up my nose!"

"I'm starving!" the embarrassed gorilla admitted. "Do you have any peanut butter?"

Although he was tempted to say, "I told you so," Bradley carefully dried his face and counted to ten. Then he got Harry a jar of peanut butter.

As Bradley handed him the jar, Harry said, "I need some bread to spread it on."

"Spread it on that fancy new mitt of yours," Bradley suggested.

"Pleeeease!" Harry begged. "Give me something to go with the peanut butter."

Bradley thought for a minute, then said, "Okay, I have just the thing. I'll be right back."

"Pickles?!" Harry whined when Bradley returned with a jar. "Who in the world eats pickles with peanut butter?"

"You will if you're hungry enough!" Bradley shouted as he slammed his door.

Harry's thoughts immediately turned to Matilda the Hippo, who lived across the street.

Matilda was sweet and generous, but at 100 years old, could no longer hear very well. Harry hoped she'd have bread and jelly.

There was no response to Harry's first knock, so he knocked harder. There was still no response, so Harry knocked even harder.

After a dozen more knocks, Matilda finally asked, "Who is it?"

"It's me," said Harry.

"Who is it?" asked Matilda again.

"It's Harry!" he bellowed.

"Oh Barry, you old rascal, it's been ages!" Matilda declared, as she opened her door.

"Why, you're not Barry, you're Harry!"

"How are you feeling today, Matilda?" the starving gorilla asked, trying to be as pleasant as possible.

"What am I peeling? I'm not peeling anything, Harry. I was warming up some grass soup. Would you like to join me for lunch?"

"No, thank you," Harry frowned, his face turning green at the thought of grass soup. "But I'd really like some bread and jelly."

"You want Ted's Deli?" Matilda asked, somewhat confused.

"No!" Harry screamed into the hippo's ear. "Can I please have some bread and jelly?"

"Ah," Matilda nodded, "Leadbelly. He was a great performer. I remember going to hear him with Grandma Hippo ..."

"Not Leadbelly!" Harry interrupted. "Not Ted's Deli!" Then as loud as he could, Harry shouted: "Bread and jelly!"

"Ah, why didn't you say so? I'd be happy to give Ted some jelly." And with that, the hard-of-hearing hippo waddled to her kitchen and soon returned with half a jar.

"Who's Ted?" she asked, as she handed the jar to Harry.

"Never mind," said Harry, giving up on getting bread from Matilda. "Enjoy your grass soup."

"What a nice boy," thought Matilda as she waved good-bye, "to come all the way here just so Ted could have some jelly."

Harry figured his last hope for a sandwich was the neighborhood's absent-minded scientist, Gertrude the Skunk.

"Who is it?" asked Gertrude, hearing a knock on her door.

"It's me," answered Harry.

As Gertrude opened her door, the worst odor you ever smelled came out of her house.

"What stinks?" Harry blurted out.

"It's my son. I'm so proud of him," the skunk announced, smiling. "He just sprayed for his very first time."

"Well, never mind about the smell," the very hungry gorilla said. "I want to make a sandwich. I have peanut butter. I have jelly. But I don't have any bread."

"But isn't bread an important part of a sandwich?" asked Gertrude very innocently.

"Of course it is," said Harry, who was now so hungry he could barely stand. "Would you please give me some bread – quickly – before I die of starvation?"

"Sure," Gertrude said. "I'll be right back."

By the time the absent-minded skunk got to her kitchen, she had already forgotten about Harry and the bread.

Meanwhile, he waited ...

and waited ...

and waited!

Finally, holding his nose, Harry walked into the skunk's smelly house. Gertrude was busily at work on her latest invention.

"Hi, Harry," she greeted him, "nice of you to stop by. I'm building a time machine. How does it look?"

"It looks like a refrigerator! Don't you remember – I came here for some bread?"

"Oh, really? Will a dollar help?" asked Gertrude, reaching into her pocket.

"Not that kind of bread, you nincompoop!" Harry said, shaking his head in wonder. "The kind you use for sandwiches!"

"Oh sure," said Gertrude, "help yourself."

Harry grabbed two slices of bread, and then, right there on Gertrude's kitchen counter, put together his sandwich.

On the first slice, he spread plenty of peanut butter. On the second slice, he emptied the jar of grape jelly. The sandwich still looked a little skimpy, so Harry even added Bradley's pickles.

He was about to take his first bite, when Gertrude's son, Petey, walked in, said hello, and proudly sprayed for his second time.

Sandwich in hand, Harry flew out of the house, gasping for a breath of fresh air.

Finally, sitting on a log at a safe distance from Gertrude's house, Harry was again ready to try and eat.

But as he lifted his sandwich for the second time, a greedy seagull swooped down and grabbed it – right out of Harry's hands.

Hungrier than he had ever been, and extremely frustrated, Harry began to cry.

Bradley, who was out jogging, saw what had happened. He felt very sorry for his best friend and put a comforting hand on Harry's shoulder.

"You probably want to say, 'I told you so,'" Harry said. "Well you were right. I was a real dummy to buy the mitt instead of peanut butter."

"Why don't you return the glove, get your money back, and buy some food?" suggested Bradley.

"I can return the mitt and get my money back?" asked Harry, in disbelief.

"Didn't you see the sign in Sammy's Store? 'Merchandise can be returned within seven days for a full refund.' C'mon, I'll give you a ride."

"Great! Let's go!" Harry responded.

In the car, Harry turned to Bradley and said, "I wish I didn't have to choose between this awesome mitt and a full refrigerator."

"You can have both! Just save a little money every week," Bradley told him. "By the time your fancy glove goes on sale again, you'll have enough to buy it back."

After returning the glove, they headed to the supermarket. On the way, Harry spotted a diner.

"Stop the car!" he blurted out. "I'm starving! Now that I've gotten my money back, I can afford to treat us to the Lunch Special, get groceries, AND still have a little left over to save."

"What'll it be, pal?" asked the waiter.

"Two double-thick sandwiches for my friend and me," Harry said. "Both with peanut butter. Both with grape jelly. And both with pickles."

"Pickles?" asked the waiter with a puzzled look on his face. "Who in the world eats pickles with peanut butter?"

Harry and Bradley started laughing, and both said at once, "My best friend does, when he's really hungry!"

The End